TWO

LITTLE

TRAINS

for Ed Emberley—G.P.

Two Little Trains

Text copyright © 1949 and Renewal Copyright © 1977 Albert E. Clarke III Living Trust
dated April 4, 2013.

Illustrations copyright © 2020 by Greg Pizzoli

Library of Congress Control Number: 2018968290

ISBN 978-0-06-267651-1

The artist used custom-made rubber stamps and Adobe Photoshop to create the illustrations for this book.
Typography by Greg Pizzoli and Rick Farley

19 20 21 22 23 SCP 10 9 8 7 6 5 4 3 2 1

❖

Newly Illustrated Edition

TWO LITTLE TRAINS

story by margaret wise brown

pictures by greg pizzoli

HARPER

An Imprint of HarperCollinsPublishers

Two little trains

went down the track,

two little trains went West.

CHUG CHUG CHUG

two little trains to the West.

One little train

was a streamlined train,

PUFF PUFF PUFF

to the West.

PUFF PUFF PUFF

One little train

was a little old train,

CHUG CHUG CHUG

going West.

CHUG
CHUG
CHUG

LOOK DOWN
LOOK DOWN

that long steel track,

that long steel track to the West.

Two little trains
came to a hill,
a mountainous hill to the West.

PUFF

CHUG

With a Puff and a Chug,
they went right through,
under the hill to the West.

Look through,
look through
that long dark hill,

PUFF PUFF PUFF

that long dark hill

to the West.

CHUG CHUG CHUG

Two little trains came to a river,

came

to

a

river

going

West.

CHUG CHUG CHUG

They went over the river to the West.

CHUG
CHUG
CHUG

below the bridge,
at the deep dark river going West.

The rain came down
on the two little trains,
on the two little trains going West.

And it made them darker,
and wet and shiny,
as they went on their way to the West.

The snow came down
and covered the ground,
and the two little trains going West.

And they got white and furry,

and still in a hurry

they puffed and chugged to the West.

The moon shone down
on a gleaming track,
and the two little trains
going West;

and they hurried along
and heard the song
of an old man singing
in the West.

LOOK DOWN
LOOK DOWN

that long steel track

where you and I must go;

that long steel track
and strong cross bars,
before we travel home.

The wind it blew,
and the dust it flew
around the two little trains
going West.

But the dust storm drew
not a toot or a whoo
or a whistle
from the trains going West.

Then the mountains came beyond the plain,

and the trains started climbing West,

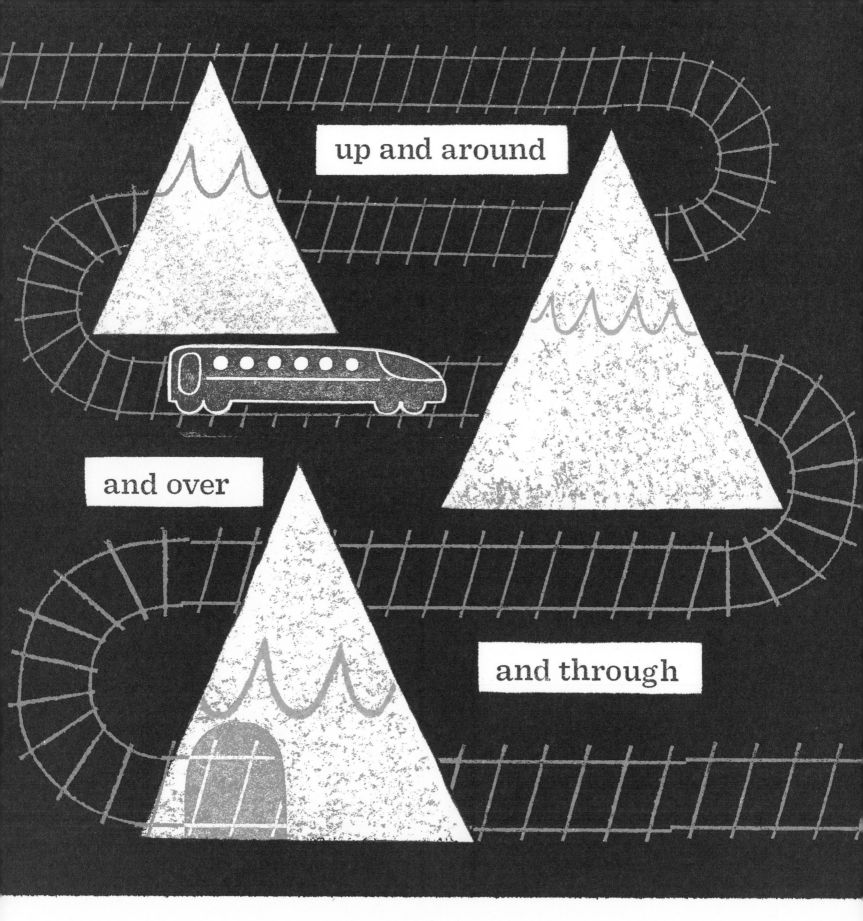

the great high mountains

to the West.

The ocean was big,
the ocean was blue,

beyond the land in the West.

And the little trains stopped.

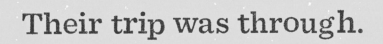

Their trip was through.

They had come to the edge of the West.